There Lives a Young Girl in Me Who Will Not Die

There Lives a Young Girl in Me Who Will Not Die

Selected Poems

TOVE DITLEVSEN

Translated from the Danish by Sophia Hersi Smith and Jennifer Russell
Foreword by Olga Ravn

PENGUIN BOOKS

PENGUIN CLASSICS

UK | USA | Canada | Ireland | Australia
India | New Zealand | South Africa

Penguin Books is part of the Penguin Random House group of companies
whose addresses can be found at global.penguinrandomhouse.com

Penguin Random House UK,
One Embassy Gardens, 8 Viaduct Gardens, London SW11 7BW

penguin.co.uk

Penguin Random House UK

Der bor en ung pige i mig, som ikke vil dø published in Danish by Gyldendal 2017
This new selection and translation published in Penguin Classics 2025
002

Set in 11/13pt Dante MT Std
Typeset by Jouve (UK), Milton Keynes
Printed and bound in Great Britain by Clays Ltd, Elcograf S.p.A.

The authorized representative in the EEA is Penguin Random House Ireland, Morrison Chambers, 32 Nassau Street, Dublin D02 YH68

A CIP catalogue record for this book is available from the British Library

ISBN: 978-0-241-63736-4

Penguin Random House is committed to a sustainable future for our business, our readers and our planet. This book is made from Forest Stewardship Council® certified paper.

MIX
Paper | Supporting responsible forestry
FSC® C018179

Contents

Foreword: Who I Ought to Be and Who I Am

While I write this, my husband is cycling through the rain, taking our one-year-old son who last night yet again wouldn't sleep, to nursery school, and I am thinking of Tove Ditlevsen's poems. I, too, want to write lists of my quirks, vices, unattractive traits, that which is me but not me. Those I love, but don't love. What I ought to do and be, but neither do nor am.

Reading these poems, which were written between 1939 and 1976, I realized that Tove Ditlevsen's poetry is always about the discrepancy between *who I ought to be* and *who I am* (which leads to the inevitable *awkward* moment in so many of Ditlevsen's poems).

Take, for instance, 'The Eternal Three', where love is not the exalted union of two souls; rather, one is always in love with the wrong person. Or in 'Self-Portrait 1', where Ditlevsen lists what she can and cannot do: 'I cannot: cook/ pull off a hat/ entertain company . . . I can: be alone/ do the dishes/ read books'. Or in 'Warning', where the heart 'can only dream, not yearn/ for what exists in light of day'. In these poems, there is so often a longing for something that is not, something that was, something that could be.

Or in the poem that lends its name to this collection:

'You had a girl's dream of a husband and baby, / and you got what you wanted but were still alone'. Fulfilling the dream of family doesn't bring an end to loneliness, it doesn't lead to what you thought it would. Instead, you're split in two – you are now the girl from before, the girl who still lives and cannot die – and the woman who is 'left roaming a world of stone'.

While I write this, the nursery school teacher gathers my son up into her arms; soon they'll hand out apple wedges to the children. While I write this, our wages trickle into our accounts, silent as snow; and while I write this, my husband cycles to his office; and while I write this, the hours race by, and I need to buy groceries, and I need to clean the fridge.

Tove Ditlevsen was born in 1917 into a working-class family in Vesterbro, Copenhagen. She attended school until the age of sixteen, after which she did various odd jobs and finally, in 1940 at the age of twenty-two, married the fifty-two-year-old Viggo F. Møller, editor of the poetry journal *Vild Hvede* ('Wild Wheat'), who had published her first poem in 1937. 'It probably wasn't necessary to marry him to move up in the world, but no one had ever told me that a girl could make something of herself on her own,' Tove Ditlevsen later said. She had debuted in 1939 with the lauded poetry collection *A Girl's Mind*, and from there her body of work grew steadily. She produced about a book a year or every other year – a staggering output – publishing thirty books and countless articles and agony columns. Meanwhile she had children and got divorced, then remarried, first to Ebbe

Munk in 1942, then to the doctor Carl T. Ryberg in 1945. In the following years she became addicted to prescription drugs. In 1949 she was committed for the first time to a psychiatric ward (she would return several times throughout her life), and in 1951 she fell head over heels in love with Victor Andreasen, an editor of the tabloid newspaper *Ekstra Bladet*, to whom she was married for twenty-two years before their bitter divorce, which figures in several poems in this book. In 1955 the collection *A Woman's Mind* was published, cementing Ditlevsen's acclaim and earning her De Gyldne Laurbær ('The Golden Laurels'), a once-in-a-lifetime prize awarded by booksellers. Her magnum opus, the memoir *Dependency*, was published in 1971 and describes her drug addiction and many husbands. The book's Danish title, *Gift*, is a homonym that means both *poison* and *married*; in this way, Ditlevsen pointed to the thin line between love and addiction, between marriage and abuse.

Victor Andreasen and Ditlevsen's relationship was turbulent and the subject of much gossip, not least in the press. Shortly after their divorce, Ditlevsen published an anonymous personal ad in her ex-husband's newspaper that read:

> Having escaped a long, unhappy marriage, I feel lonely in this world where everyone is coupled up. I am 52 years old, 172 centimetres tall, slender and blonde. I have an eight-room apartment in Copenhagen and a lovely summerhouse. I have no lack of money, only love. I've made a name for myself in literature, but what good is that when I am missing a loyal and loving companion of a suitable age, preferably a motorist. Interests: literature,

> theatre, people and domestic bliss. Please supply a photograph and details of personal circumstances.

I have always thought that the ad was such a good example of how Ditlevsen, in demeaning herself, in fact gains the upper hand. It's a tactic she uses often in her poems. The literary critic and author Niels Barfoed has described it as follows (italics mine):

> There is something unguarded and accessible about Tove Ditlevsen's person, at times even a certain do-what-you-will-with-me attitude, which can be shocking if you don't understand *that this defencelessness is her own particular form of resilience*. She's tough as nails, this woman. Accessible? Certainly. *Behind her accessibility, you sense secret areas, concealed regions not a soul can access.* Not even her. And it is naturally these places we encounter in her poetry, which is to a great extent poetry about darkness and fear of the dark, about something that lives its own life inside you, inside reality.

I can't say whether Barfoed's quote captures Tove Ditlevsen's *person*, but it's a good description of one of her *literary* strategies: using defencelessness as resilience. Behind the defencelessness there is something you cannot reach or lay claim to – do what you will, but there are parts of me you will never conquer.

Everyone knew right away who had written the ad. Ditlevsen was incredibly famous. From the outset of her career, she appeared almost weekly in magazines and newspapers, on television and radio, in articles, photo features and her popular agony column in *Familie Journalen*.

Many of her contemporaries looked down on Ditlevsen for appearing in lifestyle features, giving interviews, often posing for photographs, in the kitchen, at her desk, with her children, almost always in the home.

Ditlevsen was one of Denmark's most photographed writers. Her fame helped keep her financially afloat, because even though Ditlevsen was very popular among readers, she was always short of money (what she writes in the personal ad isn't true, or at least she contradicts herself repeatedly elsewhere). Or perhaps she feared running out. Her upbringing in a working-class family where money was always scarce had a lasting impact.

Tove Ditlevsen was not only a working-class writer, but a worker's writer. She describes the conditions of workers in Vesterbro, the daily lives of women and children in working-class neighbourhoods, the poor, the marginalized, the oddballs, the sex workers on Istedgade. In her poems, there are also echoes of working women's schlagers (catchy pop songs with often sentimental lyrics), poetry and lullabies.

Housework, childminding, care work and so forth are important features of her authorship. Her writing has not previously been considered proletarian literature, but I would like to explore this further.

The revolutionary subject, the worker, has always been presumed to be a man at the factory. But when women bring children into the world, children who grow up to go to the factory, work is being done. All the work that goes into reproducing the labour force, not only growing them from your own flesh and blood, birthing and nourishing them, but also keeping them clean and capable, keeping the hearth warm, caring for the elderly, all this is work, is production, reproductive work, and should be considered as such.

If it is the woman's job to bear children and keep house, to produce new workers for the state, feed them, keep them clean and healthy, the woman's relationship to her own body can be compared to that of the worker's to the factory. Hence, women's literature about their own bodies and housework is *workplace literature*. Tove Ditlevsen was a worker's writer.

It was with good reason that feminists of the 1970s (a group Ditlevsen never identified with; she remained in every way possible an outsider until the end) said that 'women never retire', and 'holidays and weekends are overtime'. In her 1959 essay collection *Flugten fra opvasken* ('Fleeing the Dishwashing'), Ditlevsen describes how a woman can only escape the household by having a cause greater than herself – doing charity work, becoming a nun or perhaps obeying the call to write.

In many of Ditlevsen's poems, we find this reproductive work described – the work of housekeeping and childrearing, of waiting on men and her aversion to it. While her early poems are written in formal verse, and in the original Danish are rhyming, her later work is narrow on the page and pithy in style. The ultimate shift occurs in *The Adults* (1969), which is characterized by the exhaustion and audacity that hallmark the rest of her authorship. Gone is the 'girl's dream of a husband and baby'; now is the time of divorce, of alcoholism, and no matter how experienced and accomplished Ditlevsen becomes – as a writer, a mother, a woman – she will never feel at ease with domesticity.

Her poems increasingly revolve around this feeling of unease. From her debut until *A Woman's Mind* in 1955, her poems uphold the dream of a future happiness only possible in the bosom of family, but her later poems harbour no such illusions of any possible familial harmony and instead centre on seeking brief respite: in writing, in alcohol, in childhood dreams, in death.

Ditlevsen died by suicide in 1976, at the age of fifty-eight. Photographs of her funeral procession show a sea of working-class women trailing behind her coffin through the streets of Copenhagen.

Since her debut in 1939 aged twenty-one, Ditlevsen's poetry has been dogged by the question of whether or not it was old-fashioned. Tove Ditlevsen continued to write in rhyming verse after World War Two and well into the 1960s, and this was, understandably, provocative to many, not least her fellow poets who were waging the modernist battle to challenge readers' conception of what a poem should be.

This critique of Ditlevsen was common and is perhaps best encapsulated by the author Klaus Rifbjerg's comment in a 2005 TV programme about Ditlevsen:

> She wrote rhyming poems, which were well crafted and well formulated, but wore a kind of corset she had squeezed herself into . . . She followed a tradition that goes back not only to the previous century, but the one before that, a continuation of that sort of romantic poetry where 'pain' rhymes with 'rain' and so on . . . Quite old-fashioned!

Here, too, lurks a discrepancy between how people believed Tove Ditlevsen *ought to write*, and how she *actually wrote.*

Let's talk about Rifbjerg's corset. It's an apt image: comparing fixed verse with the restrictive and constrictive garments women have been stuffed into throughout history.* In this case, it's clear that Ditlevsen has *squeezed herself into the corset* of her own volition. She has chosen this fixed form, these old-fashioned rhymes, a form of poetic, misogynist control.

But perhaps Ditlevsen didn't have the same opportunities to be free as Rifbjerg when he indirectly champions free verse as the superior antithesis of the literary corset. And one might ask whether the experiences Ditlevsen writes of have anything at all to do with freedom. Are they not precisely about a lack of freedom? About lost girlish dreams, about pain inflicted in a distant childhood, about husbands who walk out and children who look up at you strangely, and you remember once again that you are their mother?

While I write this, the nursery school children are strutting hand in hand down the path at Vestre Cemetery where Tove Ditlevsen is buried, the workers are slipping out into the sunshine after lunch, it smells of coffee, and I wonder whether the time in my life when a man will love me intensely, with no regard for children and little dogs, is definitively over.

What I'm trying to say is that some of Tove Ditlevsen's poems work deliberately with worn-out language, with sentimental language. With the corset. With the cliché. It's

* I've recently been made aware that it's a myth that corsets are constrictive, but Rifbjerg thought they were!

the voice of Eve in the eponymous poem who says: 'That's why my mouth has wilted, it has kissed too many men, / it has sung too many songs, it will never sing again.'

For me, this has always been a model of how you could write as a woman. Not the only way, but an important way. To embrace the image of the doll and speak from that position, cast aside like Eve in the poem, with nothing but old, worn songs on your fading lips.

It isn't easy to explain, but I understood it intuitively the moment I met Tove Ditlevsen for the first time, at the age of twelve, on a daybed in my grandfather's study after everyone else had gone to sleep, after I found a green book on his bookshelf and began to read.

I envisioned how she, the poet, wanders through a forest of pop songs, picking shiny, bright-red plastic apples for her poems.

These are the poems that take a form that doesn't seek originality, doesn't want to *make it new*. What do the poems want? They want to revive what has been cast off by tradition, the poetic scraps on the garbage heap. Why do they want to do that? Because using an archaic register is a working-class poet's middle finger to the hoity-toity modernists and, at the same time, a way of resurrecting discarded language. With this discarded language, it's possible to express an experience that cannot be articulated in the prevailing forms.

The preoccupation with rediscovering Ditlevsen's work has been considered, by some modern critics, as a feminist pursuit: not literary, but solely political. This is an attempt to relegate Ditlevsen's work to the field of 'women's writing', not real literature. It's interesting to see how this is linked to the capitalist ideas of 'sales and branding', as if the re-emerging interest in Ditlevsen is an unholy marriage between women's lib and some dirty capitalist spiel, where young girls, vain creatures that they are, are sold pocket mirrors in the forms of novels, poems, selfies. The devaluation of female-coded poetry is palpable.

Which leads me to this idea of the woman – particularly in Ditlevsen's lifetime – as an anachronism in society. Of society being organized in such a way that the woman must play a role she has stopped playing (housewife, beloved, beauty).

I'm reminded of a quote from Doris Lessing's *The Golden Notebook* about women's love lives: 'Women's emotions are still fitted for a kind of society that no longer exists. My deep emotions, my real ones, are to do with my relationship with a man. One man. But I don't live that kind of life, and I know few women who do. So what I feel is irrelevant and silly . . . I am always coming to the conclusion that my real emotions are foolish. I am always having, as it were, to cancel myself out.'

To cancel oneself out, to wear a corset.

If we read Ditlevsen's poems through the lens of Lessing, you could say that Ditlevsen's so-called sentimentality is a poetic anachronism that functions as a subversive tool, an anachronism on a par with a woman's emotional life.

There live girls in us who will not die.

And while I write this, all my kitchen appliances hum and spin, soon I'll have to pick up my son, and soon the chicken will need to be put in the oven, and soon I'll need to find the strength among my emotions to support my husband in his much too stressful life, and I have to condition my hair, yet again sleep only two or three hours tonight, and maybe our kid has asthma, and I write *Sorry for not responding sooner, Apologies for the late reply, I'll get back to you as soon as I can*. I don't understand how it's possible to be a mother and a partner and a worker at the same time in this society without breaking down. Let me be your canary in the coalmine, I'm about to pass out from lack of air. I am too hard to love, I am ripe for hospitalization. I cannot: arrive on time/ remember names/ make my body available at all times of day. I can: read poems/ fold clothes/ soothe my child.

The poems in this selection celebrate Tove Ditlevsen in all her power and glory. It includes all the classics, such as 'Flickering Lanterns' and 'Childhood Street'. It presents Tove Ditlevsen as a working-class poet, and features those of her poems that have fallen by the wayside, the hard-hitting, free-verse poems from the final years of her life. Above all, it shows how her authorship lays bare a woman's struggle between *who she ought to be* and *who she is*.

Olga Ravn
Copenhagen
September 2017

Notes

The quote about marrying Viggo F. Møller for the sake of being published in *Vild Hvede* comes from *Tove Ditlevsen om sig selv* ('Tove Ditlevsen on Herself'), Gyldendal, 1975.

I found the Niels Barfoed quote in Karen Syberg's biography of Tove Ditlevsen, *Myte og liv* ('Myth and Life'), People's Press, 1997. She found it in an issue of *Politiken* dated 26 March 1971.

The Klaus Rifbjerg quote is from the television programme *Store danskere: Tove Ditlevsen* ('Great Danes: Tove Ditlevsen'), produced by Mirian Mide and first broadcast on the Danish Broadcasting Corporation on 3 April 2005. (Thank you to Anne Mari Borchert for drawing my attention to the quote in her excellent thesis on Tove Ditlevsen and Ingeborg Bachmann.)

Doris Lessing's *The Golden Notebook* was first published by Michael Joseph in 1962.

There Lives a Young Girl in Me Who Will Not Die

Ritual

When I am dead, please lay me
to rest in a jet-black coffin,
and dress me in a crimson gown
with long sleeves made of velvet.

Paint my coffin dark as coal
for all the others are white,
and I'm so fair it suits me best
to lie in a jet-black coffin.

Choose a dress of the deepest red
to show I loved life dearly,
but be sure it goes to my toes,
so never again will I freeze.

Sing a hymn, if you must,
but only if you believe,
and if you wish to please me,
sing that jazz I danced to.

No drab or dreary men
shall carry out my coffin,
give me eleven choir girls
to whisk my corpse away.

And there shall be no sermons
to bring my mother to tears,
what's the point – when I was alive
I never set foot in church.

So waste your grief on another,
for though I loved life dearly,
I longed to sleep and now I rest
here in my jet-black coffin.

Anxiety

I wake up at night and switch on the lamp,
why – I haven't a clue,
there is the basin, there is the wall,
and there is the blanket, still blue.
But I am seized and swept across
turbulent waters of dread,
for something ice-cold and fated
has crept inside my head.

Come, the light is on and I'm awake,
step out of the shadows you haunt
and tell me, gruesome, almighty power,
what is it exactly you want?
Have you not any compassion?
See, I'm too tired to fight
this unsoothable fear that washes
over me night after night.

Are there seven seas of anxiety
where every single drop is bound
to drip its poison into my mind,
until love and hope cannot be found?
Are there oceans of anxiety
where every single wave
is destined to crash into me,
bringing horrors I alone must brave?

Perhaps I have been granted strength
to carry more than I can bear,
only someone condemned to death
would be so rootless and full of despair.
If I could have but one wish fulfilled
I'd return this gift I've been given,
if it costs my life and soundness of mind
I don't want to be held in its prison.

I awoke at night and switched on the lamp
to find my heart, now replaced
by something evil, slowly growing
until all goodness had been erased.
All I wanted was to sleep undisturbed
under the cool sheets where I lay,
so why am I dragged into nights with no end,
when I love the clear light of day?

To My Dead Child

I never heard your little voice,
never saw your pale lips smile at me,
but the kicks of your tiny feet,
for those I'll always rejoice.

You were all my hope, my heart's beat,
I kept you safe inside of me –
all my yearning, life's greatest dream.
Oh – your perfect little feet.

We were together for so many hours,
I shared my body with you.
Surely we cannot be blamed
for succumbing to greater powers.

Dearest, now you will never long
for life's quick pulse, for better or worse –
no matter, my boy, sweet dreams,
the weak must yield to the strong.

See how I hold your cold fingers,
grateful to be near you yet.
Quietly I kiss you, without tears,
though a burning cry still lingers.

When they arrive with the white casket,
you needn't fear, Mother is by your side.
And for the first and very last time,
I will wrap you in the softest blanket.

I'll make believe you lived a few days more,
I'll imagine that you smiled up at me,
and your little mouth suckled at my breast
until not another drop could pour.

How heavily the coffin-bearers tread,
my breast tautens senselessly for you.
Little child, my dead, golden dream,
I kiss your tiny feet – with dread.

The Cruel Years

What good's a woman once time has snuffed out
the glint in her eyes and the swell of her lips,
once the soft curve of her cheek is hollowed
and her every limb is tormented by gout.

What good's a woman once the man she embraced
below the blossoms of the apple tree
has grown fat and bald and snores all night,
the allures of his youth now laid to waste.

Once the years have passed, all those wasted springs
lost to hope that withered and hoping in vain,
once the wishful wings of her soul are cropped
and she always knows what tomorrow will bring.

Begone, evil spirits, who cruelly empty
the glint from her eyes and swell from her lips
– come loyal lipstick, and help me tell a lie,
for I wish to be forever twenty.

I Love You

I love you because your spirit flickers
like a candle left by a window.
I love you because when I think you're mine,
the flame blows out, and it isn't so.

I love you because you don't carry on
about wedding bells and vows and things,
a love like ours, so fleeting and precious,
should not be bound by any gold rings.

For I will never darn your tattered socks
or see you trudge about with a frown,
and you will never find me tired and glum,
wasting away in an old nightgown.

No, let us meet in the very late hours,
and dance, dance, while others are asleep.
Let's ask no questions, make no promises
– for promises are not made to keep.

You will only see me wrapped in bright silks,
forever aglow with mirth untold.
That way, when the time comes to reminisce,
you'll have a fine picture to behold.

Admission

The two of us must never, ever part,
listen to what I'm saying, sweetheart,
our happiness is so great, but beware,
there is only so much I can bear.

When I was a child, we once had a vase
safely kept in an out-of-reach place,
so big and heavy, artfully adorned
with fragile rosebuds and tiny thorns.

Enthralled by the forbidden and simply
because daring to do it thrilled me
I lifted the vase down and felt its weight
between my hands, so noble and great.

A curious thought crossed my mind one night,
how heavy it was, and I so slight,
though smashing it would be quite marvellous,
this desire was also dangerous.

For one endless, tantalizing second,
I fought the horrid voice that beckoned:
'Go on, now that you are home all alone,
do something for which you can't atone.'

Potent forces impelled me to destroy.
Now the world is empty of all joy.
Ten thousand shards can never be repaired.
Good angels turn their backs in despair.

– – –

Don't you see? I want you to understand:
Anything entrusted to me slips from my hand,
and so, for the sake of our happiness, my dear,
do not care for me so much, you hear!

Solely For You

A candle burns at night,
burning solely for me.
If I blow on the flame it blazes up,
blazing solely for me.
But if you speak softly, whisper sweet words,
it grows brighter than any light,
and deep in my breast
burns – solely for you.

Eve

Look at this mouth that kissed with such ardour and
zeal,
see these wounds on my lips, these wounds no one will
heal.

My poor mother taught me: it's better to give than to
take,
so I gave with willing hands, unaware of my mistake.

Just as birds fly off once the last berry is claimed,
they took what they wanted and then left unashamed.

That's why my mouth has wilted, it has kissed too
many men,
it has sung too many songs, it will never sing again.

And if I die on this night, no one will mourn or
miss me,
they loved me long ago, and not one is left to kiss me.

All my life I have hungered for the sweetness love might
yield,
but on these eager lips of mine, my fate was long since
sealed.

Wisdom I had little of, that's why I lost life's game,
and by others I was called the most horrid of names.

To the white evening star above my heart cries so sadly –
no more will these lips be kissed, these lips that kissed
  too gladly.

Moonsick –

Can it be true I've forgotten you? You, who once
were closer to me than my own heartbeat
yet became unattainable as a dream –
you, who were just like the rustle of distant trees
and the blue mountains' timeless shadows –
you, whose desire passed my soul by
and left me the joy of always pining.

I was a roadless creature; and you
gleamed with the blank innocence of stars.
The world became vast before me,
and you had no hands anymore,
no face and no eyes.
You went missing in the dark behind me,
and I carried on, down the road of eternal yearning,
down the road of eternal oblivion.

The full moon terrifies with all its pale, flooding light:
so much beauty is foreign to me.
But when the sun rises above the forests,
I turn towards the day-moon's translucence,
and when shadows flit across it
and even the faintest cloud
can hide it from sight –
when the blazing sun stalks me like a sharp pain,

and only the half-moon can soothe with night's coolness –
then grief washes over me like a tide,
and I reach out my hands
towards your forgotten face.

Winter's Night

I want to die on a winter's night like this,
when the snow is quiet as the stars,
and the relief of the cold, white ground,
still undisturbed, will never escape me.

When I am as open as on this night,
when the Earth's immense heart beats,
and in a dream that has no end,
I glimpse what will never be mine.

I want to die in ashen moonlight
awhirl with a thousand snowflakes,
they will flutter through my hands and hair
and wrap me in an icy shroud.

Not tonight when life is calling
with such sweetness in its voice,
and little sorrows are easy to forget,
the way fallen stars are forgotten.

But another night my heart sees faintly
like shadows among forest branches,
when my weary spirit is more alone
than a planet in its silent orbit.

Then there will be no before or after.
I will beg the moon to rise,
for I fear the freezing darkness,
I cannot resist its power.

The night must be perfectly quiet,
I will not taint it with my cries,
only the moon-white snow gives comfort
and can grant me the peace I seek.

Summer Night!

Copenhagen has eyes like a watchful animal,
stretching in the morning's first ray of blue,
copper spires reach for the white summer clouds
and the slumbering harbour gently rocks its tall ships.

You and me, me and you, nothing else on Earth exists –
if you want to know me, ask the green waves,
I am as reckless as they are, never knowing what I want.
The night is so warm and every sin goes unpunished.

Hush, if you listen you'll hear how close the city is:
Its saltwater breeze is my mother's voice,
my soul is the night caressing young trees.
I am good and bad and you will never forget me.

Kiss my lips and teach me what it is my heart desires.
When I laugh and when I cry, it's the waves breaking
against black ships – do you believe in love?
What do you have to lose? What do you have to gain?

I look up towards the pale branches of the birch tree,
we stand still – all is fog, a dream, pretend.
You're happy and young, and darkness cloaks you,
so only God and I can see you are alone.

A Mother's Fear

Preferably I'd like a small, tidy girl
who holds the mystery of life inside her
and night's sweetness in her mute gaze.

At her bedside I'd pray that she
be beautiful and desire nothing,
mild as the dusking wind,
born to be a mother and a mistress.

But if it's a boy with firm hands,
with defiance in his bones and a wilful mind,
then please, God, make him look to the Earth
and patiently seek out small happinesses.

But should my son see clearly,
and should you grant him the white flame of art –
then I will light candles in your churches,
I will kneel at your great altar,
raise cross after cross upon your graves,
thankful you have given him your eyes.

But if he is one to yield when pushed
and bend in the salty east winds,
a boy who yearns and lusts for the stars –
and if he's born with this craving in his soul
and this emptiness in his mouth

which frighten me more than all else –
oh, if you brand his shadowed brow
with the black mark of shame –
if you make him an artist without talent,
most wretched of all on Earth,
please, God, kill him before he sees the light of day.

Childhood Street

I

A storm rages outside – away, away,
let fall the withered leaves.
On a day like this my longing takes me
back to my childhood street.

The rain poured and the wind howled
and all those who could stayed home.
I'll never forget those endless hours,
surrounded by death and decay.

A few of us fled the boredom upstairs,
seeking refuge in the entryway,
and half-grown boys swaggered over,
laughing loudly and tipping their caps.

Then we'd whoop and shout
our cigarettes burned red holes in the fog
and night fell in the murky courtyard,
but the street was always awake.

Music spilled from the corner bar,
we stared ravenous towards its windows.
How blindly we yearned for a greedy life
lived while the city slept.

We huddled closer and gossiped
about men in suits and women in silks,
and each time the bar's door swung open
our eyes grew wider still.

And the storm wailed its lament,
and we were much too young,
and behind the dirty jokes and tough fronts,
our hearts were heavy with dread.

So we coupled up as all life does,
and the first taste of happiness was dark,
a cruel spring's awakening on an autumn night,
we have yet to escape its shadow.

Soon enough, we went our separate ways,
over time almost all was forgotten,
we shared our very first pains and joys
and haven't seen each other since.

The storm is raging – away, away,
let fall the happy and good.
On days like these my longing takes me
back to my childhood street.

II

I am your childhood street,
I am the root of your soul,
I am the steady pulse
in all that you long for.

I am your mother's grey hands
and your father's furrowed brow,
I am the fine, gauzy threads
spun by your earliest dreams.

I armed you with my fortitude
the day you were abandoned
and streaked your mind with sadness
one night in the heavy rain.

Once I knocked you to the ground,
hoping your heart would toughen,
but I helped you to your feet
and wiped away your tears.

I taught you how to hate
and showed you hardness and scorn,
I offered you these mighty weapons,
you must learn to use them well.

I gave you your vigilant eyes,
you'll always be known by them,
and if you meet a gaze like yours,
know it belongs to a friend.

And at the sound of pure notes
playing some sweeter melody,
you will find yourself missing
my harsh, insistent voice.

Did you venture too far,
have you outgrown your friend?

– I am your childhood street,
I will recognize you again.

III

I sit in the field,
lost in the summer breeze
among the grain and white clouds.
My life is a holiday,
everything is bliss,
I am at peace with all living things.

A magazine has asked me to pen
a little ode dedicated
to the courtyard children deprived of sun –
'You, man of the people,
chip in a coin and shed a tear
from the comfort of your armchair.

These frail, frightened creatures
hidden in the shadows of damp walls,
yearning for fresh air, green grass and all' –
what nonsense.
I close my eyes,
dive into the years and see:

The cobblestones of my childhood street,
me and my brothers
when we were small:
long, red-tipped noses

and hoarse, screaming voices,
playing games that were rowdy and rough.

Kicks in the shin
and tear-stained cheeks,
pinching bottles to sell them on.
Jumping the fence at Christ Church,
getting caught by the parish clerk
and slapped by big, grown-up men.

Teasing old ladies,
catching cats in traps,
drowning flies in jars of water,
making our own fun,
scruffy and up to no good,
lords in a vast, lawless land.

Getting confirmed.
'Three cheers' and 'The world's your oyster' –
six long days a week at a factory,
finding yourself a boyfriend
one Sunday night at the fair,
the hasty romance of seventeen.

Young and clumsy, fumbling
towards life's many mysteries,
holding onto some and losing more.
Onwards with the stream,
no time for complaint,
who says we must grasp what's going on?

Mute faces slide past me
like globes of light –
where to, where to –
am I the guest on this street,
where all the doors are shut
and other children skulk
in the murky entryway?

I wake up in the field
and shiver in the sun.
Where did they go? Have I let them down?
Is there no way back?
Am I forgotten, a trespasser?
Will I never find my way home?

The Eternal Three

There are two men in the world
who always cross my path,
one is the man I love,
the other man loves me.

One man visits each night in a dream
that lives in my shadowed soul,
the other waits outside my door,
I will never let him in.

One man brought a rush of spring
that all too soon blew over,
the other offered his whole life
and came away with nothing.

One man surges to my blood's song
of passion pure and free,
the other blends with the everyday
that smothers all hopes and dreams.

All women are caught between these two,
in love and truly loved – but
perhaps once every hundred years,
the two become the same.

So Take My Heart –

So take my heart into your hands
but take it gently, and understand,
this red heart – now it's yours.

It beats so calmly, it sounds so faint,
for it has loved, without complaint,
now it's quiet – now it's yours.

It can suffer, and it regrets,
it wants to forgive, and often forgets,
but never that it's yours.

It was once so strong and proud, my heart,
it never worried when we were apart,
now it breaks – only for you.

Flickering Lanterns

In childhood's long, darkened night,
burn little, flickering lanterns,
a trail of memories left behind
to guide the frozen heart's return.

Here your untamed love still shines
though lost for countless seasons,
and all you've loved and suffered since
is bounded by your reason.

Your first sorrow has the shimmer
of yearning still unsated,
it alone is etched in your heart
when all other scars have faded.

Constant as a star in spring,
your child-like happiness beckoned,
you sought it since only to find
its fervency now deadened.

Your faith followed when you went astray,
your only loyal companion,
now it dwindles in the dark somewhere,
and once more you are abandoned.

Someone may try to capture your heart
but will never quite understand you,
for you've placed your life in the lanterns' glow.
where no one will ever reach you.

Rain

Now the heart-leaves of the birch are rinsed
of old sunshine and the dust of summer days –
when the harvest moon rose late at night,
burning coolly through fevered branches,
and the wind rustled in its dry crown.

Oh, those nights, abundant with hope
and words gentle as caresses.
There they hung, covered in dust, every
aching, wrecked promise now swept away
towards the shores of nothingness.

The absentminded city meets blank stares
as it dreams in the soft evening breeze.
It can't understand the thirst of yellow fields,
but stones and people can also drink
and breathe the late sweetness of autumn.

So fall, little droplets, onto our hearts,
release summer's scent from the wet hedges,
a new freedom like surmounted pain –
heavy dreams loosen their hold, and it's as if
all bad things break when the good rain comes.

Unborn

To you who sought shelter
in one too weak and afraid,
I hum a gloaming song
of a love betrayed.

A dead lullaby rises
from this darkest day
– little life who never loved,
was never led astray.

Little life who had
no eyes, no ears, no hair,
unseen you had to die
for yesterday's prayer.

Is that you in the shadows
beyond the apple tree?
Is it you knocking
when night envelops me?

These questions echo
in my night-empty mind,
for the one who can answer
is wingless and blind.

Tonight a childless mother,
robbed of joy and grief,
clings to a dead lullaby
offering no relief.

And It Was a Night Like This

And it was a night like this,
northern and distant and young,
and the stars seemed so wise
and the moon was yellow and plump.

And it was the very first time.
How many more would follow?
My head bowed beneath his gaze,
confused by delight and shame.

And one hundred romance novels
were hidden between my legs:
they forgot time, they forgot place,
and lust was black and sweet.

My heart grew quiet and still,
and the howling winds died down,
and each little leaf, each little blade
hardly quivered at all.

But a cold silence crept through the woods,
and again the winds began to blow:
'They forgot time, they forgot place'
– then she found another.

I ended up staying with some man,
as is so often the case.
I left my heart on a well-worn path,
I have no use for it.

It was on a night like this,
I must have been seventeen –
are the red shards of my love
still there in the tall grass?

Depression

– but she is not twilight hour's woman,
when the mind quiets and sleep is near,
where longing finds a brief respite
and come night all want is locked away.

She is the clear day's grey morning cloud,
she is the patient, ponderous temptress
who waits where all roads lead nowhere
and no day is unspoiled and new.

And if you feel a coldness brush your cheek,
a chilling solitude kiss your brow,
a glimpse of wasted hours lost to time,
a murmur of unknown darkness in your mind –

then she is near, like the harsh angel of death
only wingless and without death's consolation,
and where she fares, darkness is what she reaps,
and where she treads, life no longer grows.

And what once was beautiful is hideous now –
hesitant, you walk the path she forges,
discouraged and tired like the market's last vendor
who, without hope, waits a little while yet.

Trapped in the calm desolation of her eyes,
as if sinking deeper and deeper into mud,
heavy with longing, burdened by fear and sin,
you arrive in the land of dead dreams.

My Best Time

The best time of my day
is when I am alone,
and my thoughts can grasp
a fleeting memory –
childhood's half-light falls
through bare winter branches
landing in a stripe of sun
upon my writing desk.

Here I find what is lost
to the routine threat
of things that need doing
and things getting done –
a stolen quiet settles
coolly across the room,
before lunches must be made
and dust wiped away.

And here I have trysts
of which I never speak
with peculiar friends
from last night's dream –
I open a book and find
the unforgotten page
where poet hands combed
a young woman's hair.

And I am of no use
unlike people out there,
but in my mind's dark refuge
something is renewed –
and something knotted daily
is soundlessly undone
as a branch at dawn
sways in a bird's wake.

Marriage

With recollected passion
stirred by a reminder of lost embraces,
a cool hand's delicate touch long ago,
the dreaming silhouette
of an unknown woman
against the city's neon lights –
or perhaps:
by observing a young soldier on the train
in whose bright eyes he saw
a perfectly still mind reflect his own
and fling it back undigested
in all its baffling maturity –
his senses turn towards me,
clouded by an urge to deceive.
And I, who inhabit this house so completely,
fertilizing the dust with a tenuous idea
of a life that's my own, kneeling each day
in vague prayer next to the mop bucket's
yellow-enamelled, stoic fidelity –
covertly watch his secret face,
suddenly naked, almost defenceless,
like when nature reconquers
an abandoned garden:
just a scrap of bitter tenderness
that could not thrive, unknowingly coerced
into a lawful death of love

with no demonstrable cause.
I see it pass, and remember other caresses
of unnamed sweetness, possibly even his,
but never rousing my lust
anywhere but in memory, never again.
Silently we deny, vengefully, alone,
each other's ability to awaken desire.

There Lives a Young Girl

There lives a young girl in me who will not die,
she is no longer me, and I no longer her,
but she stares back when I look in the mirror,
searching for something she hopes to recover.

There is no one else in the world she can ask:
Where are the earnest smiles, the carefree dances?
Where are my dreams and the joy of twenty?
Tell me, have you made the most of my chances?

I try to catch that pale, shimmering gaze,
try to silence her questioning refrain,
and in the depths of my heart I hear a regret,
softly dripping like the sound of rain.

'Your dreams were flimsy, child, and doomed to fail,
your innocence ruined by the truth you were told –
your budding hopes fell to the ground
the night reality invaded your soul.

'You had a girl's dream of a husband and baby,
and you got what you wanted but were still alone,
so you remained in childhood's wondrous land,
while I am left roaming a world of stone.

'It is by your sheer strength you have not died,
but live on somewhere as a faint likeness,
though I have sold your dreams for a roof and bread
and brought you pain I mistook for happiness.

'And my only salvation is feeling your voice
as a surge in my heart's languid beat –
you are my defence, my unrest and deepest comfort,
constant and true through time's fickle retreat.'

There lives a young girl in me who cannot die
until I tire of believing I once was her.
She stares back when I look in the mirror,
searching for something she longs to recover.

The Schoolchildren

They stumble along like scattered troops
every morning, come rain or shine,
milk-moustached and shaking off sleep,
perpetually small and never on time.

You recognize them by their serious eyes,
by the fog of dreams lifting from their heads,
always in a hurry, they don't notice you:
you're a faraway season they don't yet dread.

They agonize over a stain in a book,
they're tormented by a maths exercise,
and they expect far too much happiness
from becoming childhoodless and wise.

Watching them you remember how lonely
you felt in the never-ending dawn,
while every blossom slept on its branch
and the grown-ups' curtains were still drawn.

Your narrow bed, the lightbulb's dull glow,
your bedroom rancid with need;
always too small, too late out the door,
full of sadness you'll never concede.

Recognition

We sat at the bottom of night
– for it was still night's time –
and we were conversations deep,
raucous with liquor wit.

The wine sank in dark bottles
and spilled from golden glasses,
we sorted the world's problems
and set each thing in its place.

Elation flooded our hearts
and vows of friendship were made
while old memories fell like scraps
from the clothing of our past.

Our youth danced among the stars
– for now it was memory's time –
outside a spring night blazed,
virginal, tender and pure.

We sat at the bottom of night,
side by side, growing closer,
then I noticed, as I was the hostess,
that empty look on your face.

And I recognized its despair,
that false, uneasy smile,
like catching my reflection
in an unforgiving mirror.

You turned around and held
my gaze for just a moment –
I knew then that someone
had done you irreparable harm.

For you there was nothing left,
no memories save one;
it burned in you like a fire,
white-hot and unresolved.

We sat at the bottom of night,
at the bottom of all betrayal,
there a sorrow walked by
and took all our solace away.

Wordlessly we understood –
with dead leaves in our eyes and hair,
listening to the men relive
springtimes passed and gone.

But we were just a phase,
a well-trodden terrain,
outworn and done with
and fallen like autumn rain.

The Children's Eyes

I dread the children's eyes,
they always linger on me,
as if, without meaning to,
they're quietly keeping score.

All the while I am altered,
turned towards other places,
dependent on people and things
the children do not see –

and I slip into a pattern
made of threads woven daily
from actions and intonations
scarcely recognizable to me.

Their eyes store memories
like provisions for years to come,
my face sunken in depths of light,
a reflection in rippling water.

I dread the children's eyes,
I love them dearly and grieve
to think of my own parents' lives
which their child never saw.

The New Owner

Now he's gone and my mind is emptied
of old grievances and worn-out words –
it was all just something we dreamed up
and no new thoughts grow in its wake.

The life we led here was unworthy,
frayed by the grey tyrant of habit,
we both knew we deserved better, but
clung together without purpose or plan,

until we were no longer able
to quarrel – each vulnerable spot
lay exposed like a nerve in a tooth,
and parting ways was only too easy.

Now he has gone, and a defeat
is secured, sealed up and tucked away,
and all the stars have set, announcing
a day of unbroken solitude.

I miss nothing, but on this night
I mourn that there is nothing to miss.
I am a house someone has left,
soon I'll whisper the new owner's name.

Warning

You love me? Then you must learn
the strange games my heart will play,
for it can only dream, not yearn
for what exists in light of day.

It leads you down a desolate road
where brambled thickets rip your skin,
darkly humming a woeful ode
to nightly storms that rage within –

and should you stay, it closes more,
forcing your steps still further awry,
it flaps and flails but cannot soar,
and it hurts to know my heart as I.

Confession

I long for tenderness. For soft words,
from which a lasting comfort grows.
I long for a steadfast kind of love
whose bright flames will never burn out.

But I am not tender. And soft words
cannot thrive in the tracks I leave behind.
My heart taunts those devoted to me.
I pity the soul who seeks respite here.

A worm has got to my heart's root,
spreading strange guilt through my veins.
I refuse to guard the happiness of others.
My path is rugged and painful to walk.

You chose it. You will grow weary one day.
Each look of mine will land like a blow.
My sadness, concealed by scorn,
will lay your vulnerabilities bare.

So Godspeed, the path is narrowing.
Leave me with my doubt.
I long for tenderness. For soft words.
Never have I been who you thought me to be.

Deception

Unsuited as a means to fulfil
the long list of obscure expectations
the sight of me each day reawakens,
I have now become an ever-flowing
source of your bitter rage.

And you have truly been deceived.
For I remain a stranger,
trespassing, unnerving.
Except I was always so
and am not – as you believe –
altered by anything other than age,
experience and perhaps
a slightly greater resistance to
resembling the person you imagine.

For women, it's easier. We're disappointed
a little bit less, morc gradually.
Your foreignness is evident. I see
you are yourself. But I'm no better than you
at the hard kind of love:
loving other qualities than
those we lied onto each other.

So here we are. Two people. Alone.
Until a gesture as unconscious
as the flower's quiet turning towards the sun
now and then leaves my face unguarded
and revives your old, angry hopes.

You embrace me. Again you embrace the woman
who never existed to anyone but you.
Reluctantly I abandon myself,
humiliated, devastated by a ragged tenderness
for the man I no longer believe you to be.

Girlfriends

The soft-spoken friendship between women
is made of wistful reminiscing,
is made of crisp, yellow confessions
traced absently in sunlit dust.

It lives near children and must disguise
its distinct nature and scent a little.
Under the table and linen and teacups
it hides a sweetness no one may see.

Close to a kitchen, a striking clock,
and close to the husband's taut net of veins,
close to the husband himself, his heartbeat,
his deep-rooted expectation day and night –

this friendship, ardent and unspoken,
can only vibrate like a poem
carrying between its lines a want
the poet has never called by name.

Sunday

Nothing happens on a Sunday.
On a Sunday you never meet
a new love.
It's the day of unhappy people.
The boarding house day, the family day.
The mistress's most painful hours
spent picturing her lover
with toddlers on his knee
while his wife smilingly
flits in and out with fragrant trays.
A cursed day.

Things must have been different once.
Why else would we spend all week
looking forward to Sunday?
Perhaps back when we were at school?
But even then, the church bells rang
greyly like death and rain.
Even then, the adults' voices
were thin and toneless, as if fumbling
for Sunday words.

The smell of damp and old bread,
of sleep, rubber boots and chicory
drifted even then from the stairwell

and the street, which was stiff, deserted
and especially bleak –

Sunday coated us in a greasy
disappointment brought on
by unmet expectations.

But when then? Somewhere before memory,
there was happiness, an irresistible expectation
no one could yet fail to fulfil.
Back then, the church bells meant Father was home,
his moustache, his black eyebrows and the smell of
  chewing tobacco
reappeared and lingered nearby,
and perhaps your young mother's laughter
sounded more cheerful than on all other days.

It's Sunday. Never will you meet
a new love on this day.
You sit in the living room,
flat and rigid like a cardboard cutout
in the children's eyes.

They drag their feet
and argue lazily.
'We should do something,' you say.
'Yes,' says a voice from behind the newspaper.
Then you both fall silent because all the things you
  want
to do are private and forbidden
and would expel you from the other's good graces.

The church bells ring. The children's nostrils
fill with an inherited, hopeless smell.
Across their sweet faces slides
a temporary ugliness.
The gleam in their eyes
begins to wither.

But we all look forward to Sunday,
the whole week, our whole life
we look forward to hundreds
of long, pointless, eviscerating Sundays.
The family day, the boarding house day,
the secret lover's hell.
The day the adults' sickening greyness
seeps into their children and instils
the bewildering sadness
of every Sunday to come.

Growing Up

The doors they pointed at
when we asked for the exit
were always locked, or else they were
simply fake.
When they led us to a window,
the garden, the houses, the entire landscape
were painted on the inside of the glass.
They smiled in surprise
at our disappointment.

Here they were, after all. Real as could be.
Here was the living room, infected with the smell of
  childhood.
They had spewed us out, and there was only
one thing left: to grow up.
But all the while we knew,
and knew that they knew,
that their surprise and our disappointment
were not genuine. There was an open door.
There was an ordinary window.

We buried the humiliating knowledge
deep in our hearts.
They saw with aching triumph
how each day their
success grew.

Saw how we glued ourselves to them,
frightened by a look, wagging our tails to please
a patting hand.
Always alert, shuddering with delight
when they kneaded and moulded us.
Utterly forsaken the moment their attention wavered.

And since they expected it,
since it was all part of the act,
from time to time
we'd still ask,
pitiful and meek,
where the exit was.

Childhood

The picture of a child floated past them,
sat upright in his frame, smiling sweetly;
moving carefully the way he always knew,
wearily knew they expected him to.

Once again it worked. Look, their voices quieted.
The room grew peaceful. Imperious hands lowered.
Everything became clear: their naïve affection,
all their sharp, demanding simplicity.

Never disturb them. Never leave your frame.
Much was easy, but some things were never learned.
Worst were the joys they handed him, made for
  someone else,
made for a well-defined child, unadult and adored.

Worst was thanking them through the smiling mask.
Worst were their greedy eyes that wanted
whatever distant, dangerous thoughts
were sneaking through his unknowable mind.

The picture of a child stayed with them.
A fearful child never left his frame.
Happiness was merely a guest in his heart.
The deep grooves of anxiety lead back home.

Memory

My mother and father were happy. Down the street
they skipped, giddy like children lost in their own game.
And it was a Sunday. Every flagstone rang out
with the loud clacking of my father's wooden cane.

My mother was young. I never noticed before.
She wore her white linen dress and did up her hair.
As we ran through the gate to Søndermarken Park,
her laughter carried on the balmy summer air.

A rush of joy lifted from the sharp smell of grass,
from beer and fizzy drinks and slices of roast beef.
And a budding hope quivered in the summer breeze:
My mother is happy. My father sheds his grief.

I remember no other day like that Sunday.
A childhood passed. My father was quiet and grey.
My mother was always sad from that moment on,
guarding secret longings she would never betray.

Only in the memory does my heart find peace.
My mother was young, only I noticed too late.
My father was happy. And joy resides somewhere
just beyond Søndermarken Park's green wooden gate.

Atmosphere

Hazy weather, dream weather, a whole world swathed
  in fog,
an echo engulfed by silence, as if someone called,
as if someone called out in vain long ago, forsaken
like small children left alone in the middle of the night.

Silk webs like a young girl's hair between the garden
  trees,
and from far away a bird's song carries through the
  years,
through the many years of passion whose flame died
  out, and now
in this mysterious weather rekindles like a curse.

A sallow vapour from the fields, a ghostly game of tag.
Tonight a looming, nameless shape reaches for the
  houses,
comes too close to the houses, to those who live inside,
sprinkles fear into their eyes, as if a corpse walked by.

It's weather for memories, the bitterest ones we have,
for someone called to us, and we said nothing in return.
There is no peace on Earth for those who betray a
  friend.
His pain awaits us somewhere. One day we'll meet
  again.

Forty Years

Forty years old and ripe for reconciliation,
insight, understanding. But you're lucky
if the calcified and dead
lend themselves to reconciliation now. Understanding
is no longer possible. The woman
who called for you in the dark corridor
where you, aged twenty, stayed silent, then wilfully
went your bitter way,
she doesn't call anymore. It dies
in her bones, her skin. Rife
with death she understands nothing else,
and your understanding is unusable.
Nothing inside her calls to you anymore.

And even more distant: your growing child,
too big for the living room, beyond saving from
the long plague of puberty.
Besides him, the ongoing dead,
the very dear friends who left you behind.
And no one remembers the child you once were.
Forty is the age of loneliness.
Humility, resignation and insight
into things now too late to see.

The Adults 1

In the morning
longing
has come loose
from its object
and is like
a thirst
no earthly
spring can quench.

The longing is not
for anyone
in particular
life is simply
divided into a
before and after.

Before it
was good
to wake
and know
you were
only dreaming.
Now you live
inside the dream
and know that

all the adults
are truly gone
and never
coming home.

The Adults 2

It can happen
at any moment.
Your age
tightens across
your chest like a
dress sewn
for someone else.

Or your smile
washes
over them like
a tepid liquid
that dissolves
all traits
so they can
hardly locate
their own when they
move out.

Sometimes it comes
when no one sees you.
The floors slope
the doors are
made of paper.

You stand
completely still
as if painted
on the wall.
The adults are gone
and never coming home.

Divorce 1

He would
in the case of divorce
lay claim to half
of everything
he said.
Half a sofa
half a TV
half a summerhouse
half a pound of butter
half a child.

The apartment was his
he said
because it was in his name.
The thing was
he loved her.

She loved another
whose wife would
lay claim to half
of everything.

So the marriage act stated
as clearly as
two and two makes four.

The lawyer
said so too.

She broke half of everything
and ripped the tax bill apart.
Then she left for
the women's shelter on Jagtvej
with half a child.

The child was teased at school
because he only had
one ear.
Other than that,
this life too
was bearable
since things couldn't be
any different.

Divorce 2

The day he
picked up
his furniture
the frost had
left the ground
so the builders
in the suburbs
could pour
foundations
for the prefab houses.

It was a Thursday.
Spring was on its way
said the housekeeper.
There were only two of
ten little soldier boys left.
The child was upset
but contained himself.
The bookshelves were dusty
no one had thought of that.
The walls filled with wounds
as pictures were removed.

We drank a beer
with the mover.
Outside a woman

walked by
carrying a shopping bag
with green leek tops
poking out.

It was a perfectly
normal day.
We were agreeable
and considerate.
The narrow boy
walked between us
with grown-up eyes.

Pictures
on a strange wall.
A strange woman
hammers in nails.
A strange man
arrives with new
habits in his suitcase.

The frost let go.
The mittens fell
from the radiator.
A man's back
will tell you more
than he has said
in eighteen years.

Another man and
another woman
glance off

the memory.
The day was meaningless
like what you call
love.

I'll visit you
sometime
he said.
There's no reason to –
it's not
easy for me either
he said.
The mover
wiped the foam
from his upper lip.

It was a Thursday
in parentheses.
The borders around it
have already faded.
Life tastes of ash
and is bearable.

Divorce 3

Being alone
isn't easy
other people
have impatient
waiting-room eyes.
The floor pulls
your steps out
from under you.
You hold on
from hour
to hour.
A vocabulary
of about
one hundred words
was not included
in the division
of property.

The longing for
discomfort.
The lack of
strong smells.
Stale smoke
in the curtains.
The bed is
now too wide.

Girlfriends leave
when the potatoes
need boiling.

Freedom
will arrive
with the next train
an unknown
passenger
who isn't
fond of children.
The dog is
restless
sniffs at
the wrong trouser legs
will soon be
in heat.

You read
books
watch TV
register
nothing
are suddenly
very happy
in the morning
and miserable
by nightfall.

It's a phase
your girlfriends say
something you have

to get through.
Weightless as an
astronaut
you float
in empty rooms
and wait
for the freedom
to do
what you
no longer
want to.

Divorce 4

Husbands
fill up
the whole world
block
the horizon
take charge
make
decisions
are everywhere
never call
on Sundays.

In the evening
they come
creeping
with a bottle
of cheap sherry.
You let them in
in droves
and try to
distinguish one
from the other.

They are fat
or thin
vertical

or horizontal.
They ooze
tenderness
and good advice
in return for your hastily applied
helplessness.

With domineering
cheerfulness
they fry eggs
afterwards
stuff themselves
flush the toilet
repair the TV
tell bizarre anecdotes
about their children
pull the wife
out of their wallet.

You clean up
after the last one leaves
sweep up pipe tobacco
smooth out the dent
in the pillow
go to bed
are alone
have had enough
and start over
tomorrow
in the hope of
one of them

someday becoming
distinct
and different
and calling
on a Sunday.

The Family

The family
breeds rampantly.
It moves
in clumps
and on principle
one never strays
from the flock.

It knows all.
It disapproves.
It is offended.
It monopolizes
every holiday.

Your daughter's
parents-in-law
always give the
more expensive gifts.
The phone rings
off the hook
each morning.

No stranger
would barge in
on you
the way your sister-in-law's

sister does
the day you dare
to have a private life.

You're folding the laundry.
The kitchen door opens.
She offers advice
on how to get rid of
foot warts.

She says
your brother's marriage
is not a happy one.

There is no cure
for family.
It knows you
too well to
love you
and too little to
care for
your company.

The deaths are few.
The births numerous.

All conventional
emotions
are presumed
true.

What's Hard

Being a mother is easy.
Giving birth was a breeze.
Marriage and divorce
only put a few cracks
in the plaster
like when the train
rushes by.

It's easy to write
easy to read aloud
from your own work
a good reason to
get away from home.

What's hard
is the chit-chat
afterwards.
The other adults who see
your hands shaking
and your lukewarm interest
in the subject.

The girls have baked
the cake themselves.
The principal talks
about the class trip.

It's only
half past eight.
Your stomach rumbles loudly
during a pause.
Your mouth waters
and driven by a simple
need to survive
you imagine
what the eager father
with the eye contact
and the many questions
is like in bed.

It never ends.
Your youngest is only
nine years old.
You weren't
warned in time.

The parish council chairman
is a vegetarian.
He thanks us for
a riveting discussion
and gets lost
in prepositions.

With fanatic eyes
he drinks his gruel.

He hasn't smoked
in thirty years.
He takes

pollen tablets
and doesn't vaccinate
his children.
He sneezes and smells
of garlic.

People are relentless.
They drink coffee
by the bucket.
It smells of disaster.
Childhood tumbles out
of the cupboards.

Half-mad with thirst
you set out on
the wild waters of conversation.
Everyone laughs you are
a clever dog.
Why do women
never have heart attacks?

The pastor's dentures
rattle
when he speaks.
Next time I want to
marry a pastor.
Next time
I'll bring a hip flask
and down it
on the toilet.

Rain

It always rained
on Istedgade.
The lamplight
spread
like big sunflowers
in the falling
darkness.

Down at the train station
the whores came out
looking like rich ladies
with umbrellas
and high heels.
You'd imagined them
differently
and were disappointed.

The stink from the
slaughterhouse
wasn't as bad
as during the day.
Drunk men
aren't dangerous
your friend said
child molesters
are always sober.

Policemen patrolled
two by two
white batons swung
loosely from their belts.
Their wet helmets
gleamed.
They looked alike
they knew that
you stole and sold
bottles from the lumberyard.

Danger
wafted from
the alleyways.
Unemployed men
walked home
with determined steps
and after-hour eyes.
Rowdy apprentice boys
queued up
by the cinema.

Now all the other
children are at home
eating dinner
you had told
a lie you were
a little scared
and excited
nothing happened
when you stuck together
and avoided sober men.

If you set foot
in Café Charles
you'd get killed.
Many went in
but no one
ever came out
alive
according to the
seventh graders
and everything they said
was true.

It's still raining
on Istedgade.
Nothing has changed
shuddering you pass
Café Charles knowing
you're more likely to hear
the truth from kids
than adults.

Anxiety 1

Anxiety is old
it smells of childhood
it has no object
is summoned by looks and words and
sudden noises
lives in recurring dreams where
the man you love
lays bare the murderous hatred he
conceals by day.

People's eyes are yellow
they are too close together and
have no lashes
above them the
menacing brows
unstoppably knit
the mouth's corners
drip down like wet watercolours
do not look at them
slip out of every
waking danger.

Wrap yourself in the comfort
of old forgotten rhymes
seek refuge with the troll
and the dragon the

pure evil
shun all caresses even
the child's who plays
and strokes the cat
shun his expectations
his memories
his thwarted future.

Seek their company
those peacefully turned backs
who want nothing from you
libraries waiting rooms
and railway station halls
people with a suitcase
in their hand have
solid outlines
unknown
destinations in a
world you are not part of.

All the others are transformed
in your eyes
as if unsettled by waves
they know that you see
their secrets
and innermost thoughts
they hate you lie in wait
you do not know the day
of the catastrophe that
approaches hour by hour.

Anxiety is old your
father and mother are
comfort and danger
staring through your
beloved's eyes
they are not dead.
Don't look at them put
flowers on their grave turn
on the lamps at night
clasp your hands and hum
the bygone songs
like an awful incantation.

Anxiety 2

Misery is not
disease and death or
abrupt change.
Anxiety extends far beyond
any conceivable fear.
Undetected and dangerous like
multiplying cells
it lives inside you and is nourished
by routine and habit.

Faces melt
and dissolve
if you don't avert
your penetrating eyes.
The mirrors won't be used
you cannot know
what they reflect when
darkness and silence fall.

The apartment you live in has thin
sloping walls.
A hard, sharp voice
strikes like a whip.
No reconciliation is possible.
Through his eyes
stare the adults who know
you have seen their fear.

Love

It'll end
the adults say
it won't last.

She knows
she doesn't know
she loves
his walk
the way he
runs his fingers
through his hair
his patting
of pockets
to check if he has
forgotten anything
his laugh
his voice
that drags
his accent
that thickens
when he drinks.

She doesn't understand
how people can be
happy without
knowing him.

Love is
a disease
one day she will
detest
his walk
the way he
runs his fingers
through his hair
his patting
of pockets
to check if he has
forgotten anything
his laugh
his voice
that drags
his accent
that thickens
when he drinks.

Nothing
is new
she doesn't learn
from experience
she loves
she nests
she buys two
of everything.

She feels elated
at the sight of
the two
toothbrushes.

She sees everything
through his
eyes
she feels
with his
nerves.

She pastes in
photographs
frequently visits
his mother
studies the room
he grew up in
signs a
deed
with him
the larch trees
shiver
in the night wind
she knows
the adults are right.

She is happy
she is raving mad.

With No One –

With no one
can you share
your innermost
thoughts.
With the most
important things
in life
you are alone.

It is a continuous
burden
it is a quiet joy
that here
no one can
reach you
and no one
is let in.

When I Have Time

The woman upstairs
borrows a cup of flour
to strike up conversation.
She smells of whisky
she's a widow
her son's an addict.

Sure I say
while I worry.
He didn't come
home last night
there's someone else
I don't know
whether we'll split the bills
right away.

Her mouth
is open and wet.
The words fall
onto the floor
I stuff them
back in
without looking at them.

She's unhappy
age takes its toll

it must be difficult
I say
and give her a gentle push
so the door will close.
Flour sprinkles
onto her faded
housecoat
a thread of blue silk
catches on her nail.

When I
have time
when things
fall into place
when I've had
a good night's sleep
and donated to
Friends of the Elderly and
Save the Children
I'll check in on
the woman upstairs

who no longer
needs flour
who no longer
makes gravy
and bakes white bread
who needs someone
who is happy
and has plenty of time.

The Line

There is a line
that separates those who
have liquor in the house on
Monday morning
and those
who don't.
The border-women
have hidden
four beers in the oven
where no man
would think to look.

The others meet
at six o'clock
at the grocer's.
No one gives themselves away.
There are chief physicians
alongside housekeepers and wives
with little foresight.

Sun. Pentecost. Porous
erasure
trembling hands.

You buy:
a loaf of white bread

a litre of milk
two cream puffs
and before I forget
six beers the builders
are coming today.

The shopgirl is suntanned
and has x-ray vision.
Health youth infatuation
eight hours of sleep.
You shrivel up
with your former face
your cold sore
your all too frequent
menstruation.

You carry your handbag
so the bottles don't clink.
The sun stings.
You can't get anything
right.

See-through and
guarding your breath
you wake the schoolboy
whose grown-up eyes look like
the shopgirl's.

Self-Portrait 1

I cannot:
cook
pull off a hat
entertain company
wear jewellery
arrange flowers
remember appointments
send thank-you cards
leave the right tip
hold onto a man
feign interest
at parent-teacher meetings.

I cannot
stop:
smoking
drinking
eating chocolate
stealing umbrellas
oversleeping
forgetting to remember
birthdays
and to clean my nails
telling people
what they want to hear
spilling secrets

loving
strange places
and psychopaths.

I can:
be alone
do the dishes
read books
make sentences
listen
and be happy
without feeling guilty.

Self-Portrait 2

Once you've had
a great joy
it lasts forever
hovering at the edges
of your anxious
adult days
hushing inherited fears
deepening sleep.

The bedroom was
an island of light
my mother and father
were painted
on the morning's wall.
They handed me a bright
picture book
and smiled at
my effusive joy.

I saw that they were young
and fond of
each other
saw it for the first
for the last time.
I was five years old

when everything changed.
Since then
the world has been
split into a before
and after.

Self-Portrait 3

I cross
the street
and hear
the church bells
ring. It's eight o'clock.
I want to run
but can't.
My feet are
too heavy
my legs
are limp
my heartbeat
panicked.

I see
other children
walk in pairs
two and two
towards the door
where the vice-principal
is ensuring order.
They are from
another world
they have pious eyes
my brother's old coat

is stiff and itchy
around my neck.

I run as though
underwater.
The church bells
clang.
Fear rips itself loose
from the memory.

I don't know
what happens when
you're late for school.

I wake up
adult in my bed
soaked in sweat
my heart regains its rhythm
slowly.

I know
I was never
late for school.

All anxiety leads back
to something that never took place.

Self-Portrait 4

On my childhood street
lives an old woman
who remembers me
as a little girl.
I was unruly
she says
the whole building shook
when I bounded down
the stairs from the fourth floor.

This picture of me
inserts itself
and distorts
like when
a photograph is taken
on top of another.

I fear the place
I hold in other people's
memory. They remind me
of things I have forgotten.

They stole
my face
before it was
worn out

and wear it often
on top of their own.

I don't remember
the old woman
from my childhood
the grown-ups were all the same
and ageless.
She knows something
about me she won't divulge
a secret I've never told.

It fills her up
and keeps death at bay
she tells lies and intends
to outlive me.
I never took the stairs in bounds
I was a quiet child.
I hate her.

Longing

I long
to age
to languish
and calcify
for taste buds
only roused
by strong
spices
for eyes that
only see
the brightest
colours
and ears that
only hear
the loudest
din.

I long
to forget
all of life's sorrows
for feelings
to pale
and cling to
the dead and
gone
no one

else remembers
and no one
can touch
or do
anything about.

I long
for brittleness
and aches
in every bone.
Protection
against every kind
of desire
until the day I die.
Protection
against the blood's
cursed wrath
and the white agony
of missing someone
which plagues
my weary back.

How long
life yet
feels
on these
spring nights
with their
sweetness
taunting
she who is
alone.

Oh let me
age quickly
and desire
nothing
and never again
be desired
by anyone
but death.

Once

Once:
a room
a typewriter
a job
an alarm clock
a loneliness
a hope.

Now:
an apartment
a summerhouse
things
a husband
three children
status
friend
lover
housekeeper
neglected
graves
hairdresser
psychiatrist
money
complication
lack of
joy.

Good things come
to those who wait
my mother said
longing and
understanding
came to her
too late.
She died in
the nursing home
knowing
no one.

People misunderstand
each other for
the most part.
She had
beautiful hands.
Unnoticed
life slipped away.

Reception

While they
still strangely
inflated
gnash their teeth
at the photographer
whose mouth is filled
with names
like a seamstress's with pins –
in this foyer
overcrowded
with once-a-year celebrities
so many of whom
are dead
as one guest remarks
with no small measure
of satisfaction –

the overwhelmed little
debut author
with the round elbows
hesitates on the threshold
sidetracked by the full-page
advert in the paper
as she listens to
the sweaty publishing director's
speech for the defence

wondering whether
he'll remember
to mention her name
already alien
to herself –

there she waits
with untarnished
dreams
of being admitted
into the circle of
ageing celebrities
over thirty.

The slyest of them
who swallows up
each aspiring new talent
in whom something
is emerging
demeans this
lately so serious child
with his lethal
affability –

he who knows
that a review
of twenty lines
awaits her
a month after
publication day
places his decrepit arm
around her slight shoulder

to the delight of
tabloid readers.

Thus temporarily
disarmed
she stumbles home alone
in the much too small
shoes bought for the occasion –
this little aspirant
whose steps are pulled out
from under her –
she who still feels
that the Earth is turning –
enviable and
vulnerable
still convinced fame is
something other than being
scattered and dissolved
and having the stones of one's
foundation disarrayed
by the invasive
crowds.

And those of us who know
do not warn her.
We remain
in the foyer of the dying
far too busy
tending to more important
connections.

The Others

When I push them out
the front door
they get in through
the kitchen.
They're everywhere
like discarded sentences
that think themselves too good
for the rubbish bin.
They invoke
some non-existent
distant relation
or spiritual
affinity.

Though they have stolen
my name
the authorities deny me
a new one.
The police deny me
protection.
The locksmiths
don't have time.
I'm not healthy enough to be
committed.

The dentist is
in Tenerife.
My skeleton
joins forces with
the enemy
because not even it
has access to
the round room
with doors and windows
painted by
a great artist –
someone happy whose name
no one knows.

To Someone Over With

You rough approximation
who required
all that noise
and numbed yourself
with distractions
you corrupter of
promising beginnings
with your condescending
sympathy –

You meticulous replica
of a painting that burned
in the museum
strangers set fire to
(how you once
loved the original
and the old master
whose life slipped
by unnoticed
he who suffered so
greatly at the end
and refused
all relief
because he wished
to experience his
well-prepared death

with dignity
and a clear mind) –

You who long
ago it was possible
to love;
there, at the forest inn
where the morning bird
with its yellow beak
pecked at breadcrumbs
in our hands –

From your hastily spent
youth I have extracted
a fine essence.
You will never again
disrupt my
tentative and earnest
beginnings.

For V

My evil heart rejoices
when yours is struck by grief.
It skulks just like the jackal
and eyes your every step.
It wants to see you suffer
for it has suffered too.

My evil heart knows too well
longing shows no mercy.
Every day it's ripped apart
just thinking of your name.
It searches for you vainly
in the arms of strangers.

My evil heart understands
this will be repeated.
The grief you wrought upon it
will die and fade away.
It knows forgetting's bleakness
and hates that just as much.

Soon enough, my wretched heart,
so worn and so weary,
will forget the many scars
it suffered at your hand.

It trusts it will love again
a heart that is not yours.

But the comfort of this truth
is stained with betrayal.
For grief is like the traitor
for whom we break our bread.
More bitter than grief itself
is its disloyalty.

Lola

My name is Lola.
I died,
technically,
by my own hand
at the women's shelter where
like in all other places
I was always on the run.
Two girls helped me
keep the life-savers at bay
for a certain price.
But since I was always
short on money
it was their contempt for me
that decided my fate
and I was spared waking up
in the toxicology clinic
where they couldn't
stand me either.

I never stayed long
here in the closed ward
because I smashed all
the potted plants
even though I wasn't crazy.
I felt terrific
for as long as it lasted.

A haze of red
washed over me
when the alarm rang
and the orderlies from the other
wards
came running
and grabbed me
with an enthusiastic rage
that stirred the only form
of love
I was able to feel.

By some miracle I turned
twenty-six.
To die is to lose the desire
to destroy what
others hold dear.
I come from a formidable home.
It took twenty years of hard work
to break through the safety net.
Everything flourished
under my formidable mother's
tireless care
even the potted plants
in the conservatory
that is, except one.
She tried everything,
gave it many chances:
sun, shade, warmth,
water, fertilizer, flattery.
It refused to thrive,
it wilted

withered
perished –
until finally she gave up
and tossed it in the cellar,
where, freed from obligation,
it burst into bloom
to nobody's delight.

The walls here are stained
with suffering.
I helped the lunatics
hold on,
helped them mitigate disaster
using peculiar tactics
so exhausting
they wore their faces out
prematurely –
again and again
the equally exhausted
chief physician had to
procure them new ones
through social services.

For a whole month
I shared a room with Kirsten
who every night had to punch
her pillow
one hundred and twenty times
five times in a row
so her mother
wouldn't die.
They operated on her brain

and when she woke up
from the anaesthesia
she went right back
to punching her pillow.
We congratulated ourselves
as if we had really
outwitted
all those formidable doctors.

Mostly people fled
from my life
as if from a house on fire.
I felt no remorse
and no loss.
The pain I caused others
was nothing compared to my own
despair over
the impossible demands
made of me.
Even the hunchbacks and
the harelipped
for whom I did it for free
demanded something more
something they'd never ask
of a regular whore.

Here thcy always sent me
to therapy
to knit
a never-ending dress
for a daughter
I've never seen.

Now all of this stuff
is unimportant
in light of
the only real thing
that ever happened to me:

Someone shouted my name
through the deafening
noise which soothed my fear
of being found out.
He became clear
to me.
'Poor Lola,' he said,
and understood everything
without contempt for
the deformity within me.
He too was formidable
but also a poet.

He gave me a book called
Start Writing!
full of empty pages.
In it I glued the photograph
of the napalm-bombed girl
with arms outstretched
like wings that cannot fly.
For hours I have stared at
that photograph
not feeling a thing.
Below it I wrote:
What about the photographer?

Next to her a picture
of the young man who put
a kitten in a bread slicer
and cut it up like
a loaf of rye bread.
His seeming
amusement
only made me
envious.

'Brave Lola,' said my friend
seeing all my efforts –
just as futile as Kirsten
who still punches her
pillow –
just as mad or as
meaningful.

He gave me a reason
to die happy
which would have made
all the regulars
howl with laughter
down at the local
where I had to pay twice as much
as the others.
It couldn't be
helped.

There wasn't enough stuff
in the world anyway
not enough brandy

not enough makeup.
No drink in the world
could slake my thirst.
When he realized this
he kissed me for the first
and only time.
'When you're dead,' he said,
'I'll buy a hat
and visit your grave
on a Sunday morning.
I'll stand there for a moment
all alone
and mumble a few
words only intelligible to me.'

I know he kept his promise
once my formidable family
got out of the way.
After the service
while my snivelling mother
recalled the time
I bit her nipple
until it bled
so tears blood and milk
frothed at the corners of my mouth,
the only man ever
clear to me
in my life
stood with his hat in hand
and whispered to himself
the words unsayable
while I was alive

for anyone who wished
to survive.

Goodbye Kirsten,
goodbye potted plants –
To die is to lose
the punishing desire
to destroy what
others hold dear.

Children

My heart loves all the most impossible children,
those no one cares for and no one understands.
The liars, the thieves, the promise-breakers,
the children all adults love to reprimand.

I care not for those flowerbed children who thrive
in neat rows and are strangers to want and shame.
The children whom adults dotingly trim into shape
and who can in good conscience call God by name.

The ones who know love best are those who never met it.
The sinner knows more of virtue than most would
  assume.
I loathe the pruning shears upstanding adults wield.
Wild bushes are where the rarest flowers bloom.

Tiptoer

Always standing
on tiptoe
to look out
of your
adult eyes
only too aware
of the creaking
in your stretched
skeleton
requires many
distracting jokes
so those who fill
their bodies out
effortlessly
will rupture
the perilous silence
with their
awful laughter.

It can be endured
as all tiptoers know
for only a few hours
at a time –
then you must seek out
some secluded hideaway
typically a toilet

that can be locked
from the inside.

There you
put on spectacles
to fool
the empty eye sockets
and are free
to lower down
onto your heels
finally relieving
the utterly
overstretched skeleton
whose narrow
pelvis
you vow
never again
to subject to
the foreign
bones
of fat
wilful
foetuses.

Slouched over
you recuperate
one foot below
the affronted face
you have stolen from
a far more
faithful owner
who now wears

the face of her dog
though no one
notices –
not even herself.

Then another
exhausted tiptoer knocks
on the door.
Loyal to your own kind
you straighten back up
despite the residual
growing pains
of childhood
toss the spectacles
and stare soulfully
through adult eyes
before pulling the chain
and with astonishing
bravery
you return
to those effortlessly
upright people who
fill their bodies out
and politely
pretend that
nothing ever happened.

Departure

Homesickness before departure
old anxiety
pried open.
My poor mother
to whom nothing
she wanted
to happen
ever happened
my mother with her hands thrown up
towards the low ceiling:
'That's it, I'm leaving!'
she yelled and terror
clung to my heart
like a wet rag.
The smell of dishwashing and sleep was
sweet and already
a future comfort
it lives on
in my nostrils
like the smell of grass
stays with children
born in the countryside.

I am like a tree
whose branches
are softly weighed down

by birds landing
in the abandoned nests
of others –
dear to me were the
forgetful birds who fled.
The storm of memory blew through
my autumn hair
the forester drew
the mark of death on my trunk,
I hear the chopping of his axe
grow louder each day.

Homesickness before departure
the familiar feeling
of anxious anticipation
the increasingly distant smell
of dishwashing and sleep –

the marked trees in the woods
know they will be cut down
and all the birds will leave
the empty nests.

Morning

Wake up miserable
at three in the morning
in my narrow
winter bed –
withered leaves
in my matted hair
and chips in the blood-red
nail varnish left over
from summer's
sandal days.

The taste of ash on my tongue
an aching lower back
a mean grumble
in my tooth.

Hostile furniture
of the past
refuses
the new inhabitants'
unfamiliar hands.

Old sentences
in the curtains
words the deserter
forgot

when he hastily
extricated himself –
fragments
that don't fit.

Out of step with
the season
tangled up like a
ball of yarn the cat
has played with
I stroke its
bony shoulder blades
which tremble
in its sleep.

No more birds to hunt
no mice to scare
no way out of memory's
labyrinth.
Quietly life runs out
like water down a drain.

The Round Room

Stretched to the breaking point
by uncontrollable consequences,
trapped in the insurmountable
like an unwanted pregnancy,
I can't help but wonder whether all this
was really necessary?
Couldn't one have made do
with very little;
the detail of a detail
hardly anything at all
something like a coffee tin
with a lid that fits
and slips soundlessly into place
in this world of
poorly made objects?

All wholes
are too overwhelming
a whole person is
too much to take
improbable, unbearable.
All the screws and bolts
are loose or missing
and the spare parts
were used up in childhood.
Angry mechanics who dropped out

before their apprenticeship was over
skulk about, convinced
the desire to pare myself down
targets them.

Things rattle and clink
and fall apart –
children flew out of me
like rubbish down a chute
fat and overflowing I gave up on
locating the fault
and all the plumbers
arrived too late.

Tiredness runs through my veins
I, soon used up, in whose house
little strangers accumulate
in carelessly pushed-together beds
repeatedly replaced with
new ones without footboards
so they can grow unimpeded
in their sleep.

With immense effort
I break the water
of my undesired life.
A loud splash
fills the world.
We're downsizing I tell
the nosy neighbour
and retreat
to a perfectly round room

bringing only the necessities:
a coffee tin whose lid fits
and slips into place
without a sound
to my endless delight
in the unbroken silence
I have craved all my life.

To a Little Girl:
Posthumous Poems (1978)

Crabs

Though the heavens and no small number
of not-yet-dead men can attest
to my sparing no effort
on selfless attempts
to gain first-hand experience
with every imaginable dire and dreadful disease
below the belt
purely for the benefit of humankind
and literature
I merely managed to acquire
a bout of unremarkable (albeit severely itchy)
crabs
which I only got rid of
when I broke up with the purveyor
who proved to be some sort of middleman
dependably procuring new supplies
whenever the old ones had drowned
in strange potions
which I paid innocent children
to fetch from the pharmacy
while I scratched myself to bits
in a nearby stairwell.

We found the expression 'sleeping together'
just plain silly.
There was never any sleep involved,

nor any bed.
There were stairwells, alleyways, privies,
bushes and a single (needleless) haystack
during an eight-day holiday.
And when finally years later
something akin to a bed came
into the picture,
the magic had
worn off.

Crabs have no shame in life.
When things get too perilous
in the fiery trenches
they move up to the armpits
or seek refuge in the eyebrows
whose harsh climate can only be endured
thanks to strong familial bonds.
Here my sharp-eyed mother spotted them.
'I see,' she said simply.
'You can tell that fellow
not to set foot in this house.
And while we're at it
don't you dare
come home pregnant either.'

And I didn't,
but not for lack of trying.
I wailed with disappointment
each time I got my period.
All my children were, oddly enough,
conceived in a bed.
That's how they got those stern, upstanding eyes

which made me feel guilty
about my scandalous life.

Their lives are largely a mystery to me.
But I don't think they've ever had crabs
at least I've never seen any crawling about
in their pristine eyebrows.

Early On I Evaded –

Early on I evaded
my mother's caresses
(she who was caressed by no one)
because her hands that day
smelled of dishwashing.
Hurt and confused
she withdrew, hasty as she was,
and gave up once and for all
on the work of loving me.
Like all proletarians she suffered
from toothaches often and cared
very little for men.

Twelve years old
hopelessly in awe
I watched her
leave for the carnival
repelling the ambush of old age
dressed up as an 'Eighteenth-Century
Coachman' which earned her
a bad reputation
in the neighbourhood where only men
had the right to go off the rails.

She died knowing no one.
Her bewildered hands crept

across the blanket
as though searching for something
that no longer existed.

I always scrubbed my hands with nice soap
after doing the dishes
but it was no use.
The smell was inherited
and my children abhorred it.

– All my darling runaway children
who rest easy knowing
there is time for remorse
between the stirrup and the ground.

The youngest of them
a timid contemplative
quiet-seeking boy
was fond of his grandmother.
Love often
skips a generation –

Foremother

The unrelenting
consequences of
mixing fluids
in stairwells alleyways
parks back seats of cars –
romance infatuation
heartache tears
fleeing footsteps
unknowable men's
resolute backs –

The bland smell of
neglected children
growing children
illegitimate children
remembered children
wanted children
switched-at-birth children
multiplying children
children-in-law
grandchildren
new beginnings
continuations
mucus tears
abortions
the touching courage

of survivors
in cold waiting rooms –
their lovestruck hearts'
lack of insight.

(The lonely old folks
who understood the simplification
having ultimately
set things in motion
now devoutly feed
the stray cats
that always live
near the poor.)

Phasing out
pulling back
deep contemplation –
pushing aside all
except one:

The unviable
uncontinuing
great-grandchild
whose enormous head
wobbles towards the door
to the dream of
the round room.
Gently I lift up
the little neuter
who smiles when you
stroke its left cheek.

With this age-old child
in my arms
the memoryless
conclusion to my exterior
life's staggering
coincidence
I depart
into the night
stroking
its left cheek
bringing about
a timid smile
that was worth
all the effort.

Well-Versed in Yearning –

Well-versed in yearning
and practised at losing
I am less skilled at simply
holding on to a person
who takes up all the space
staggers around the house
with a head body and arms
and an inscrutable urge to
stay or leave.

A person is too much
I cannot cope with
what's behind his brow
that is only sometimes smooth
what unexpected memories
are in his eyes
what smiles yet unborn
are behind his teeth.

Who would dare to fall asleep
with such a stranger in the house?
I have eliminated sleep and speech
and a readable expression
well-versed in yearning
and practised at losing

I often wish he would leave
and so become
distinctly near.

Afterthought

When a woman writes
little devils swarm
her most productive years
as well as men whom she only manages
to love badly and from a distance –
at the heels of those who are,
with some difficulty,
still possible to fend off
the grocers, the butchers, the bakers,
the postmen, the milkman,
the playwrights,
the lewd telephone voices,
the exam-sitting children and the singing
housekeeper who requires
coffee and chit-chat
for one hour every morning.
All this in spite of
grants meant to secure
artists
peace and quiet
to work.

When a man writes
he finds himself a true
handmaiden of art
who keeps everything and everyone

at bay when he is struck by
holy inspiration.
THE WORK is worth
all the effort
though he too loves
badly and from a distance.
On the first page
he immortalizes his
handmaiden with the words:
'Without the tireless help and care
of my beloved wife
this book would never
have seen the light of day.'

The opposite would be
ludicrous and unthinkable.
Besides getting entangled
in Women's Lib
I see only one
possible solution for
hard-working women artists:
they must be sterilized
at the age of fourteen
and subsequently placed
in soundproof cells
at one of those nursing homes
where they don't
kick the elderly
in the shins.

For some years a daily dose
of sodium carbonate will be

necessary to keep
the libido in check.

This solution has only one flaw:
even a childless woman's
never-touched breast
can fill with milk –

Translators' Note

The poem 'There Lives a Young Girl in Me Who Will Not Die' describes an older woman looking at her reflection in the mirror, only to be confronted by a girl, the ghost of her younger self. It's an image that gets at the heart of Tove Ditlevsen's life and writing: 'No experiences later in life can erase those of childhood. As a child, one sees everything for the first time, and all that comes after is only repetition,' she once wrote. The poems in this collection are full of echoes, full of memories, and they all in some way lead back to childhood.

This selection opens with poems from *A Girl's Mind*, her debut poetry collection from 1939 and the very first book she published, at the age of twenty-one (though she claimed to be twenty to seem extra precocious!). From here, we follow the 'young girl in me who will not die' through the years, through the eight collections excerpted in this book which span Ditlevsen's entire career before arriving at her very last poems, written by a poet at the height of her fame and prowess, three years before her death in 1976.

In the poems, we encounter the dreaming, playful voice of the fledgling poet who first began writing in secret as a child, and trace its development into the luminous, astute voice of a woman embittered by ageing, persistent depression and turbulent divorces. As her work evolved, it remained characterized by her vulnerability, brutal honesty and humour, as well as her ability to distil the complexities of a woman's interiority into lingering images.

In order to capture this range in our translation, we first had to unhear the insistent voice that is Tove Ditlevsen's immense legacy in Denmark. It is a voice familiar to us from required primary school reading, from well-worn quotes in wedding speeches, from catchy '80s pop renditions, from recitations by all the many people who know her poems by heart. We had to remember what it was like to read her work for the first time. Only then could we encounter the poems anew, as they are, and hear them clearly.

Tove Ditlevsen's poetry is deceptively simple and subtly masterful. For much of her career, she resisted the free verse of modernism in favour of rhymed verse in a neo-romantic style, which grew increasingly complex over the years, employing intricate rhyme schemes and syllabic patterns. Despite these strict constraints, her poems often feel effortless and natural. To render the effect of each poem in translation, we had to consider what to sacrifice and what to privilege: the images, the rhymes, the rhythm . . . When making these choices, we let the poems guide us. Some poems lent themselves to rhyme; at other times the specific words and images felt too important to let go of in favour of the rhyme, and so we focused instead on syllables and/or metre to lend them structure. In many ways, each poem in this collection is the result of compromise; not only as a labour of co-translation, created through intense collaboration, mutual inspiration and concessions, but also in terms of capturing the complexities of the original.

As you move through Tove Ditlevsen's oeuvre, you will see her style shift – very obviously, on the page, and also in tone and style. The hymnal, more traditional stanzas in which much of her early work is written become less regular, more enjambed, grow less fixed in their form, and, correspondingly, in their rhythm. Rhyme becomes increasingly less common, less conventional punctuation is used, until finally we arrive at the succinct, incisive lines of free verse she wrote towards the end of her life. But as her style shifts over the years, what remains constant are the familiar repetitions that echo throughout. Like a chorus throughout the collection, certain words repeat again and again: Child, night, heart, eye, life, man, mother, adult, hand, woman, dream. These are the simple building blocks that make up her poems and provide the foundation upon which she builds the haunting imagery and complex existential themes that pervade so much of her writing: neglect and need in childhood, its lasting effects, all the balms one seeks out to soothe these earliest wounds, like love, sex, drugs, hospitalization; the inescapable shame, anxiety and depression; the allure of motherhood, marriage, and the resistance to it; the yearning for escape through writing and death.

So often, the poem's speaker longs for *tydelighed* – the quality of being clear. Our translations of *tydelig* each capture a different aspect of the Danish: clear, readable, distinct, well-defined, evident. This yearning for *tydelighed* is further emphasized by the many faces and eyes that permeate this collection: stolen faces, worn-out faces, melting faces, faces sinking into depths of light, forgotten faces, mute faces, a dog's face you wear as your own, faces as masks that can be taken off or kept on, indefinitely. The eyes in the poems watch you, see right through you, or into your soul: grown-up eyes, pious eyes, penetrating eyes, greedy eyes, upstanding eyes, your children's eyes, your beloved's eyes. Herein lies an awareness of being watched and observed, of having one's secrets exposed, of being judged and found lacking, but crucially also a desire to be seen and to see others clearly. Several of the poems embody a longing for people to appear sharply outlined and therefore decipherable and within reach. Despite this, Ditlevsen often writes from a place of remoteness; she is an accustomed outsider and makes this role her own by casting herself as an observer in her own life, appearing again and again as a stranger to those closest to her.

Throughout her life, Ditlevsen retreated to her 'mind's dark refuge'. In her final collection she gives this sanctuary a form: the round room. It's a quiet room only she has access to, where she is free of domestic and maternal obligations, where she can be most herself and keep melancholy at bay, though the price of entry is loneliness, estrangement and an absence of love. Here, she can retrieve her childhood memories, recollect and reflect; here is where she can write. Though Tove Ditlevsen wrote in an array of genres, and though her memoirs are widely considered her magnum opus, she saw herself first and foremost as a poet. Brought to tears by the hymns she read on her first day of school, poetry became her way into writing. By her own estimation, poetry was also where she excelled: 'All my life, I have loved writing poems most and am – with few exceptions – convinced that I have done my best work in my poetry.' In these poems, we find the young girl, the images and the themes upon which all of her work rests. In her poetry, her writing begins.